Timeless Fairy Tales

Aladdin and His Magical Lamp

AWARD PUBLICATIONS LIMITED

A long time ago in China, there lived a boy called Aladdin. His father had died when Aladdin was just a baby, so his mother had to bring him up alone.

Aladdin and his mother lived in a tiny hut on the outskirts of the city. In the distance they could see the many roofs of the Emperor's palace.

Aladdin's mother was one of the Emperor's washerwomen. Aladdin did his best to help his mother: he would collect the bundles of dirty laundry from the palace for her to wash. When the laundry was clean and dry, he'd take it back to the Palace.

Sometimes, he would get a glimpse of the Emperor's beautiful daughter, whom he liked very much. Aladdin would see her walking in the palace gardens. But it is unlikely that she ever noticed him.

Although Aladdin and his mother worked hard, they were very poor. The roof on their hut leaked when it rained, and at times they barely had enough rice to eat.

Aladdin often dreamed of having a beautiful house, and he promised his mother that one day they would have a palace of their own! But his mother just smiled. Aladdin also dreamed of marrying the Emperor's daughter…

One day, while Aladdin was out walking, he met a stranger, who said to him, "Your name is Aladdin."

"That's right!" said Aladdin, surprised. "How did you know?"

"I am a magician!" said the man. "And with my magic I can give you and your mother all the riches you ever dreamed of."

This is just what Aladdin had been longing to hear. "I would like my mother to live in a fine house," he told the magician.

"Of course," said the magician. "But first you must do something for me. There is a secret cave in the mountains, and in it is a precious lamp. I want you to go into the cave and fetch the lamp for me."

Only the pure in heart could enter the secret cave; that is why the magician had sent Aladdin.

The cave was full of many treasures! Just for fun, Aladdin tried on a golden ring, but when the magician saw this he hissed, "Quick! Give me that lamp, or I'll shut you in the cave forever!"

"No, please help me out first," insisted Aladdin. "Then I'll give you the lamp."

But the magician was furious. He closed up the cave, leaving Aladdin inside.

"I'm trapped," thought Aladdin. "There's no way out. I'll never see my poor mother again!" Aladdin sat down on the stone floor in despair. He twisted his hands together and as he did so he rubbed the ring on his finger. It was a magic ring.

There was a puff of smoke and a figure appeared before Aladdin.

"I am the Spirit of the Ring," said the figure. "What is your wish?"

"Please take me home," begged Aladdin. "And let me take the precious lamp with me." In an instant, he found himself back at home.

Aladdin put the lamp in his mother's room. Then he went out into the garden to await her return. He still had the magic ring on his finger, so he wished for a glimpse of the Emperor's daughter.

The Spirit of the Ring granted his wish.

Just for a moment he had a vision of the Emperor's daughter walking in the Palace gardens, and it seemed to Aladdin she was more beautiful than ever.

Later, when Aladdin showed his mother the lamp, she said, "It doesn't look very precious to me. And what is more, it needs a jolly good clean." So she went to the drawer and took out a cloth.

As Aladdin's mother polished the lamp, there was a bright flash of light followed by a loud bang, like a clap of thunder! A huge golden figure appeared before them, saying, "I am the Genie of the Lamp. What is your command?"

Aladdin's mother was amazed!

"It's a magic lamp! Now I know why the magician wanted it," said Aladdin.

The Genie of the Lamp waited while Aladdin and his mother thought of something to wish for. Finally, they asked for great riches, a grand house with servants and good food to eat.

"And make sure the roof doesn't leak," added Aladdin.

"Your wish is granted," cried the Genie. In a flash, Aladdin found himself dressed in silk, and his mother in the finest satin.

It wasn't long before Aladdin invited the Emperor's daughter to tea.

They fell in love, and one day Aladdin went to the
palace to ask the Emperor if he could marry the
Princess. He took the Emperor a gift of gold and
silver. The Emperor, who also liked Aladdin, gave
his consent to the marriage.

Aladdin and his Princess settled down and lived
happily together in Aladdin's palace.

Then one day, the magician returned. He was dressed as a pedlar, shouting, "New lamps for old!" It was a trick to get the precious magic lamp.

Aladdin was out, but a servant girl heard him call.

She brought down the magic lamp, which looked quite old, and exchanged it for a shiny tin lamp.

As soon as the magician saw the lamp, he knew it was the magic lamp from the treasure cave.

"At last I've found it," he said. "How Aladdin escaped from the cave I will never know, but now I'll turn him into a laundry boy again." Saying this, the magician rubbed the lamp...

When the Genie of the Lamp appeared, the magician said, "Take the Princess, Aladdin's palace, and me, to Africa!"

"Your wish is my command," said the Genie. Aladdin's palace, with the Princess and the magician inside, flew high over the sea until it landed in Africa.

"This will teach Aladdin to meddle with magic," said the magician, laughing. "When he sees that his wife and his palace have vanished, he'll wonder if he's been dreaming!"

When Aladdin came home he discovered that his palace had disappeared into thin air, and his Princess was nowhere to be seen.

He sat down and tried to think. He could not understand what had happened. Perhaps it had all been a dream after all?

Then he remembered the magic ring that was still on his finger. So he rubbed it, and the Spirit of the Ring appeared.

"What is your wish?" asked the Spirit of the Ring.

"Please take me to my Princess," said Aladdin. And away they flew, high above the sea…

The Princess was overjoyed to see Aladdin. "I never thought I'd see you again!" she cried.

Aladdin asked her what had happened.

She explained, "The magician has got the magic lamp. He made a wish, and we flew here from China. It was most amazing!"

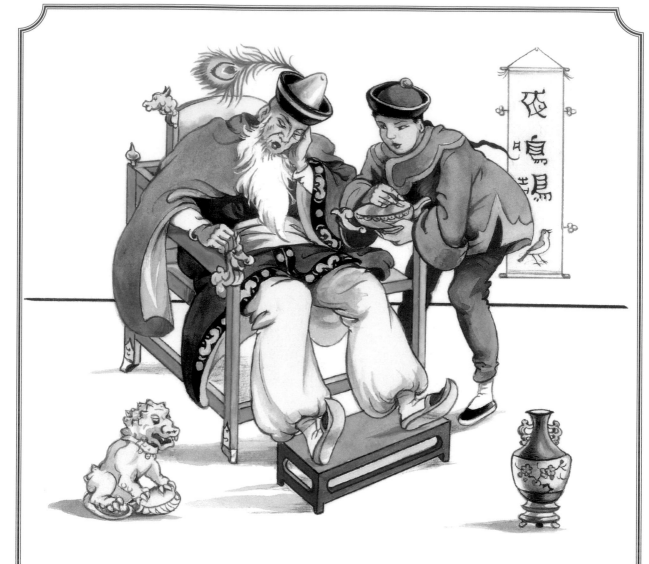

Aladdin hid until the magician was asleep.
Then he crept up and took back the lamp. When he
rubbed it, the Genie of the Lamp asked once again,
"What is your command?"

"Take the Princess, the palace, and me back to
China," said Aladdin.

"What about the magician?" asked the Genie.

"Please leave him here," said the Princess.

The Genie of
the Lamp granted
their wish.

Immediately, Aladdin
and his Princess were
back in their palace in
China. The first thing
Aladdin did was to
hide the precious lamp.

When the magician woke up, he was all alone in the desert in Africa.

"Oh dear!" he sighed. "That's the trouble with magic: it's not very reliable!"

THE END